D0374883

Put Beginning Readers on the Right Track with
ALL ABOARD READING™

The All Aboard Reading series is especially for beginning readers. Written by noted authors and illustrated in full color, these are books that children really and truly *want* to read—books to excite their imagination, tickle their funny bone, expand their interests, and support their feelings. With four different reading levels, All Aboard Reading lets you choose which books are most appropriate for your children and their growing abilities.

Picture Readers—for Ages 3 to 6
Picture Readers have super-simple texts with many nouns appearing as rebus pictures. At the end of each book are 24 flash cards—on one side is the rebus picture; on the other side is the written-out word.

Level 1—for Preschool through First Grade Children
Level 1 books have very few lines per page, very large type, easy words, lots of repetition, and pictures with visual "cues" to help children figure out the words on the page.

Level 2—for First Grade to Third Grade Children
Level 2 books are printed in slightly smaller type than Level 1 books. The stories are more complex, but there is still lots of repetition in the text and many pictures. The sentences are quite simple and are broken up into short lines to make reading easier.

Level 3—for Second Grade through Third Grade Children
Level 3 books have considerably longer texts, use harder words and more complicated sentences.

All Aboard for happy reading!

For Melody, Jon, and J.B.—F.J.

For Ross the Boss—M.S.

Special thanks to Abby Popper, program administrator, Recycling
Office, Westchester County; and to Kevin Conklin, supervisor,
Westchester's Material Recovery Facility—F.J.

Text copyright © 1996 by Francine Jacobs. Illustrations copyright © 1996 by Mavis Smith. All
rights reserved. Published by Grosset & Dunlap, Inc., which is a member of The Putnam &
Grosset Group, New York. ALL ABOARD READING is a trademark of The Putnam & Grosset
Group. GROSSET & DUNLAP is a trademark of Grosset & Dunlap, Inc. Published
simultaneously in Canada. Printed in the U.S.A.

Library of Congress Cataloging-in-Publication Data

Jacobs, Francine.
    Follow that trash! : all about recycling / by Francine Jacobs ;
illustrated by Mavis Smith.
        p.   cm. — (All aboard reading)
    Summary: Describes how metal, glass, plastic, and newspaper trash
can be recycled.
    1. Recycling (Waste, etc.)—Juvenile literature. [1. Recycling
(Waste)   2. Refuse and refuse disposal.]   I. Smith, Mavis, ill.
II. Title. III. Series.
TD794.5.J33   1996
628.4'458—dc20   95-41963
                                                                      CIP
                                                                       AC

ISBN 0-448-41314-0 (pbk.)   A   B   C   D   E   F   G   H   I   J
ISBN 0-448-41601-8 (GB)   A   B   C   D   E   F   G   H   I   J

ALL
ABOARD
READING™

Level 2
Grades 1-3

Follow That Trash!

All About Recycling

By Francine Jacobs
Illustrated by Mavis Smith

Grosset & Dunlap • New York

Every day you throw out
about four pounds of trash.

So does everybody else

in America!

In a year

that's 180 million tons—

enough to fill a line of garbage trucks

halfway to the moon!

But after you
put out your trash,
what happens to it?

Getting rid of garbage

is a problem.

Most trash is buried in places

called landfills.

But landfills fill up.

They are ugly

and dangerous, too.

Some leak poisons

that pollute our water.

Yuck! Who wants to drink

water that can make you sick?

Some people are trying

to pass laws to stop landfills.

Trash is also burned in incinerators.

(You say it like this: in-SIN-er-a-tors.)

Incinerators make lots of smoke.

Some of the smoke is poisonous.

Pee-U! No one wants to breathe

that smelly stuff!

KEEP OUT

Burning trash also makes

soot and ashes.

Soot makes our clothes dirty,

and our faces, too!

People don't want incinerators

where they live.

Would you?

Is there a better way

to get rid of trash?

There sure is!

Recycling!

Recycling means turning things
that have been used
into new things.
Much of the trash we throw away
can be recycled.

This sign means
the bin is for recycling.

Nature recycles what it grows.

Dead trees and plants rot.

They go back into the earth

to make new soil.

People recycle scraps of food

such as apple cores and banana peels.

They use them
to fertilize gardens.
The scraps help flowers
and vegetables grow.

But nature can't recycle everything.

If you drink a can of apple juice,

what happens to the can?

Metal cans are not so easy

to get rid of.

Neither are things like
glass jars, plastic bottles,
and newspapers.
That's why you keep them.
Then you take them out
on special days—
recycling pick-up days.

Look!

Everybody's trash is in bins

out on the curb.

The bins are full

of glass jars,

plastic bottles,

and metal cans.

Next to them are piles

of newspapers.

Soon a truck comes by.

It collects all the things

to be recycled

from every house.

But where does the garbage

go from there?

It goes to a recycling plant.
Here trucks tip their loads
onto the "tipping" floor
of a huge garage.

In one part of the garage,

the trucks tip loads

of glass, plastic, and metal.

In another part,

the trucks tip loads

of newspapers.

Mountains of trash rise up!

Wow!

Imagine wasting <u>all</u> this!

And somewhere

in that great, big mess

is your small pile of trash.

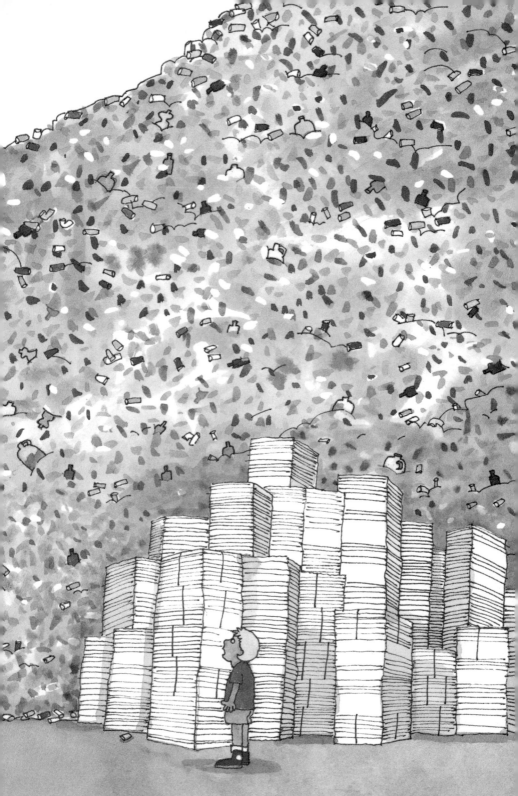

A tractor shoves

the glass, plastic, and metal

onto a moving belt.

Things that don't belong there—

like laundry baskets and lawn chairs—

are taken off.

They could break the machinery.

The belt moves on.

It passes under a strong magnet.

Whomp!

The magnet pulls up

steel cans used for soup,

vegetables, and other foods.

Then they are dropped into a bin.

The rest of the trash on the belt

goes through a great shaking box.

It is like a big sifter.

It shakes out small pieces

of glass.

They fall into another bin.

They will be crushed

and used to make roads.

The belt keeps on moving.

It moves under a blower.

<u>Whoosh!</u> There is a big blast of air.

The air blows the light aluminum

and plastic things

onto another belt.

Glass bottles and jars
stay behind.
People sort them by color—
green, brown, and clear.
Each color glass is crushed
and stored in a separate bin.

The aluminum and plastic
get separated too.
The aluminum cans
are dropped
into a machine.

It flattens and packs them
into tight bundles.
These bundles are called bales.
The different kinds of plastics
get crushed and packed
into bales, too.

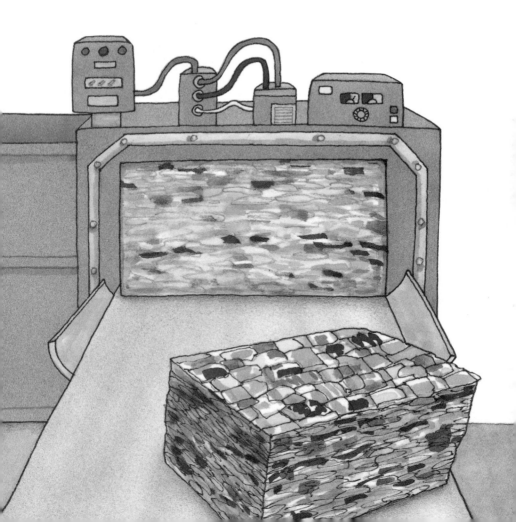

But what about

all those newspapers?

Do they just stay

on the garage floor?

No!

The newspapers

go on another belt.

At the end of the belt—

swish!—

the newspapers fall and flutter

like autumn leaves.

They tumble down into a machine

that packs them into bales, too.

All the trash

is sorted and packed now.

There are big bales of steel,

aluminum, plastic, and newspaper.

There are huge bins of brown,

green, and clear crushed glass.

Trucks wait to take it all to factories.

There it will be made

into brand-new things.

What happens to steel cans?
Some are melted down
and made into new steel cans.
Recycled steel also becomes
toys, trays, and lunch boxes.
Recycling old steel costs less than
making new steel.

What happens to aluminum cans?

They are melted, too,

and made into new cans.

Can you imagine

80 BILLION aluminum cans?

That's how many are used

each year in America!

But the empty soda can

you throw away today

can be made into a new can

and back on a store shelf

in only six weeks!

Aluminum is also used to make

bicycles, canoes, tennis rackets,

and lots of other things.

What happens to glass?
Glass is melted down
to make new bottles and jars.
Like aluminum and steel,
glass can be recycled
over and over and over again.

What happens to plastics?

Soft, clear plastic is melted

and made into bottles

like the kind soda comes in.

It is also used to make carpets

and warm linings

for snowsuits and sleeping bags.

42

Harder plastic is turned into
trash cans, pipes,
and plastic lumber.
Plastic lumber is strong and heavy,
just like real wood.
It can be used to build fences,
playgrounds, and park benches.

What happens to paper?

Newspaper is shredded
into tiny pieces.

These pieces are mixed with water
and turned into a gloppy paste.

It is called pulp.

Pulp is pressed and rolled out
to make new newspaper.

But newspaper can only
be recycled a few times.

After that it falls apart.

Paper is the largest part
of our trash.

Besides newspapers,

there are magazines,

phone books,

cards,

letters,

books,

and more.

And where does all that paper

come from?

Trees—lots and lots of trees!

Not every piece of paper

can be recycled.

But if everyone in America

recycled just their Sunday newspapers,

500,000 trees could be saved each week!

Recycled paper can be used

to make paper towels, posters,

and cardboard for egg cartons,

cereal boxes, and game boards, too.

Everything you put out

to be recycled

comes back again.

Look in your room

for recycled things.

Then you can tell your parents,

"This used to be trash!"